For the Sheape family—Glenn, Caro, Josh, and Amanda

Baa Baa was here

First U.S. edition 2016. Library of Congress Catalog Card Number 2015936913. ISBN 978-0-7636-8066-4.
This book was hand-lettered. The illustrations were done in pencil and rendered digitally.
Candlewick Press, 99 Dover Street, Somerville, Massachusetts 02144. visit us at www.candlewick.com.
Printed in Shenzhen, Guangdong, China. 16 17 18 19 20 CCP 10 9 8 7 6 5 4 3 2

CANDLEWICK PRESS

Baa Baa SMART SHEEP

Mark Sommerset

illustrated by Rowan Sommerset

Little Baa Baa was bored.

I'm bored.

When along came Quirky Turkey.

"Oh, no . . .
it **IS** poo!"

Little Baa Baa was bored.

I'm bored.

When along came Silly Billy...